Fairy Tales: The Origins, History, and Interpretations of the World's Most Famous Fairy Tales

By Gustavo Vázquez-Lozano & Charles River Editors

A 19th century depiction of Tom Thumb and the giant

About Charles River Editors

Charles River Editors is a boutique digital publishing company, specializing in bringing history back to life with educational and engaging books on a wide range of topics. Keep up to date with our new and free offerings with this 5 second sign up on our weekly mailing list, and visit Our Kindle Author Page to see other recently published Kindle titles.

We make these books for you and always want to know our readers' opinions, so we encourage you to leave reviews and look forward to publishing new and exciting titles each week.

Introduction

Gustave Dore's sketch of Mother Goose reading to children

Fairy Tales

In the early 16th century, when Europe was coming out of the Middle Ages and Germany was divided into several kingdom states, a girl named Margaretha von Waldeck was born in Hesse, a region of the German Empire covered by thick forests. Margaretha was the daughter of Philip IV of Waldeck, a nobleman marginally remembered in history books for advancing the Protestant Reformation in his domains. The Count had a daughter with Margaret of Frisia, but as in any era, wealth and a good name were not a guarantee of happiness: the Waldeck family owned copper mines (where misshapen and malnourished children worked; people called them "dwarfs"), but Philip's wife died four years after giving birth, leaving behind her daughter Margaretha. The child was breathtakingly beautiful according to testimonies of the time.

Shortly after being widowed, Count Philip married again, this time to Katharina of Hatzfeld, whose portrait is still preserved. The red-haired woman had short curly hair and —at least in the portrait that is available— a nasty grimace in her slightly off-centered mouth. And she hated the girl. At 16 she forced her to go to Belgium, where Margaretha met and fell in love with the son of the king of Spain, the future King Philip II, who was captivated by her beauty. The Spanish prince was six years older than Margaretha. When they began their brief romance, he was 22 and she was 16. The fairy tale ended in 1554 when Margaretha was poisoned by Spanish agents, who saw the impending marriage and considered that politically she had nothing to offer to Spain. The same year of Margaretha´s death, Philip ascended the throne. Proof that the girl was poisoned, writes German historian Eckhard Sander, can be seen in her testament, written hastily with shaky handwriting, as if she were trembling in agony.

Dense forests, evil stepmother, beautiful girl, dwarfs in mines, a prince and, eventually, poisoning (in that order). Sound familiar? Most will recognize the basic plot of Snow White and the Seven Dwarfs, one of the most popular fairy tales in history. Even if the passing of time (and Disney) embellished it with a thousand details, in particular the happy ending, this and other tales reflect the Sitz im Leben or setting in life in which fairy tales emerged. The stories, which were transmitted orally during the Middle Ages, are like fogged windows to the way of life, the kind of people and social conditions of the regions where they took their final shape. In some instances, such as Snow White and the Seven Dwarfs, they may be echoing historical facts. And the poisoned apple? Sander thinks that the lethal fruit was added later, during the stage of oral transmission, in remembrance of a man who really existed in Germany and was arrested for giving poisoned apples to children because he thought they were stealing from him.

For centuries, beautifully illustrated fairy tale volumes have rested innocently on kids´ night tables around the world, long ago relegated to the dubious honor of being branded as "children's literature." But every story is a file packed with information, and Cinderella, Snow White, Puss in Boots and Bluebeard have always intimated that perhaps they have more to tell besides "beautiful" stories, the same ones that animated the minds of several generations of children. Whether or not they had peaceful dreams is another matter, because even in their current versions, sterilized and with their original contents doctored, classic fairy tales are far from innocent stories for five year old children. Snow White, Cinderella, Sleeping Beauty and Rapunzel are full of violent jealousy between mothers and daughters, families so poor that they have nothing to put in their mouths, infanticide, tedious work, illicit sex, and traces of old religions. It is no wonder that fairy tales were originally collected without children in mind. It was only later, with the arrival of illustrators and then cinema, that they began to become the virtually exclusive domain of underage readers.

Like in the secret room where Bluebeard kept his dead wives´ bodies, or the enchanted forest one should not venture into, fairy tales conceal not only historical events and the depiction of the hard lives of people in the Middle Ages, but according to psychoanalysts, they are also a mirror of truth where people's desires, fears, illicit appetites and flaws are encoded. Snow White's stepmother had a good reason to be so upset when the mirror finally told her who she really was.

This classic moment in literature is an excellent metaphor of what fairy tales are as a genre. Until recently they were still relegated to the book shelves of the youngsters; lately they have been studied seriously by scholars of the most prestigious universities in the world, successfully exploited by the entertainment industry, and even banned in some schools.

Fairy Tales: The Origins, History, and Interpretations of the World's Most Famous Fairy Tales is an invitation to peek into the history of fairy tales and see humanity reflected in them. The image they throw back may not always be the most satisfactory, but for better or worse, it'll be the one societies have to face. Along with pictures of important people, places, and events, you will learn about the history of fairy tales like never before.

Contents
About Charles River Editors..2
Introduction..3
   Once Upon a Time...There Were Hundreds of Kings 7
   A Literary Genre is Born 13
   A Certain Father Had Two Sons...17
   In Search of the Historical Characters 22
   Fairy Tales from Other Kingdoms..28
   The Interpretation of Fairy Tales 40
Bibliography 42
Free Books by Charles River Editors 44
Discounted Books by Charles River Editors 45

Once Upon a Time...There Were Hundreds of Kings

"Will you give me your youngest daughter?" said the White Bear;
"if you will, you shall be as rich as you are now poor." - East of the Sun & West of the Moon

The origin of fairy tales is lost in remote antiquity. An anthropologist recently found evidence that the several versions of *Little Red Riding Hood* branched a thousand years ago from a common narrative of the 1st century AD.[1] Others, like *Sleeping Beauty*, published by Charles Perrault, have clear antecedents in older stories like *Sun, Moon and Talia,* published 60 years before in Italy. But Talia's story itself is derived from older traditions that were told around the fire during the Middle Ages.

> **Comment []:**
> Pauline Erlinger-Ford 10/16/16, 8:53 AM
> Usually the name of a fairy tale is italicized. The same comment applies to the other chapters as well.

> **Comment []:**
> Pauline Erlinger-Ford 10/12/16, 6:15 PM
> It is known by many as "Sleeping Beauty" without the "the." So I will change it through this piece.

Perrault

---

[1] Jamie Tehrani, a UK scholar, analyzed 58 variants of the story around the world. The anthropologist believes that Little Red Riding Hood evolved from a story called The Wolf and Children that circulated orally about a thousand years ago.

Regardless of each tale's ancient origins, it was the publication of *Histoires ou contes du temps passé*[2] by Charles Perrault in 1697 that marked a turning point in the history of the genre, which to date is alive and well. Perrault was a member of the French Academy who wrote literary adaptations of stories circulating the same among rural people and society salons. His book with 11 stories (eight in prose and three in verse) became an instant success that brought recognition to Perrault at his 70 years of age, although hardly any modern parent would want to read the first printed version of *Little Red Riding Hood* to her children. In Perrault´s 1697 version, the wolf orders the "village girl" to climb into bed with him, and after a brief comic dialogue which highlights the masculine characteristics of the animal, the wolf devours her. Some early versions of the tales of the Brothers Grimm, published a century later, are even more lurid.

The Brothers Grimm

Fairy tales coexist in the literary world with mythology, fables and legends, but they all have a distinctive hallmark. They all belong to folklore, but fairy tales don´t insist on a moral teaching

---

[2] Stories of Fairy Tales from Past Times with Morals or Mother Goose Tales.

like fables, and often times even if there is one, it´s not so clear. This way, the stories leave a lot of room to the imagination. Unlike legends, fairy tales don´t involve historical figures or aspire to verisimilitude, as is the case with the Robin Hood or Davy Crockett narratives, and fairy tales don´t occur at defined places, such as the numerous legends about the streets of Mexico City. Unlike myths, fairy tales are about regular folk and don´t seek to explain the origin of the cosmos or cultural practices.

Fairy tales contain magical elements (such as shoes dancing by themselves or shape-shifting beings), recurring themes and recognizable characters, most notably wicked stepmothers, fairies, dangerous forests where horrors lurk, magic objects, and lots of prohibitions. With a few exceptions, they all have happy endings; poverty, oppression, confusion or dangers are overcome, and good and hope triumph over cruelty and melancholy.[3] This convention is so universal that to say something turned out to be a "fairy tale" means that the result was impossibly happy, or that expectations were so high that only a miracle or a magical intervention could have made them come true.

Since the dawn of mankind, storytelling has been a crucial activity to forge group identity and express ideals, fears and desires. Not surprisingly, there are several theories about the origin of fairy tales, including that they are residues from mythology or ancient polytheistic religions, that they all come from India (where they were composed before the common era), that they are small creeds of the first agricultural societies, or that Perrault invented them to entertain the Parisian aristocracy, but their true origin remains a matter of speculation. Interestingly, the recurrence of certain elements (a specific economic, geographic and social context) speaks to people of a setting in life that accounts both for characters and plots. In this regard, the most popular fairy tales as they are now recognized probably originated in Europe sometime in the Middle Ages, specifically in the centuries after the fall of the Carolingian Empire in the 9th century AD. Why during the Middle Ages? Stories like *Sleeping Beauty, Rapunzel, Snow White* and *The Princess and the Pea*, with their abundance of kings and castles who seem to be at a stone's throw, with their impenetrable forests and extreme poverty as a rule, reflect the conditions of Europe a few centuries after the fall of the Western Roman Empire. That period was called, a bit ironically, the time of the "loss of comfort."

The fall of Rome in 476 AD brought a sharp decline in the living standards in Europe, malnutrition, disease, and the collapse of the imperial infrastructure that began to be buried literally under new forests, not only in Italy but also across the continent. The Roman Empire had discovered the strategic value of deforestation to carry out its conquests. In times of the naturalist Pliny (23-79 AD), Italy lost its forests almost entirely. After the fall of the empire,

Comment []:
Pauline Erlinger-Ford 10/12/16, 6:21 PM
Who refers to the kings but cannot refer to castles.

Comment []:
Pauline Erlinger-Ford 10/12/16, 6:20 PM
A stone's throw from what?

---

[3] A notable exception to the rule is the original ending of Little Red Riding Hood: the wolf eats the child.

woodlands dominated again. This process involved the loss of influence of the Church outside the cities and the reappearance of old beliefs in the countryside, imported by the northern tribes. Economic specialization and literacy fell too, because education had been previously financed with Roman taxes. The destruction of efficient Roman roads also meant a decline in trade. The return to primary economic activities allowed only the subsistence of the local population.

On top of all this, wave after wave of barbarian invasions from northern Europe brought new groups into what were once Roman dominions. Borders were no longer safe and the forests became dangerous places. In the territories of what is now France, Spain, Italy, Britain and Germany, new rulers —"strong, rude people"— became kings of weak states without professional armies. This process continued for hundreds of years, giving rise to hundreds of small principalities that barely communicated with each other. Walls and castles —an essential element in fairy tales, perhaps more than fairies themselves— began to appear. Castles were a European innovation. Their massive construction began around the 9th century AD after the disintegration of the Carolingian Empire and the division of the territory among several lords and princes.[4] "The weakening of centralized authority created an environment in which fortifications built by noble families ultimately came to flourish." (Creighton, 2005).

Archaeologists have found that the spread of castles began in France around the Loire valley, and then to the Rhine in Germany, and westward to England and the rest of the island. An extreme case was the center of Catalonia, Spain, where a castle was built every 15 square miles on average. At first they were simple structures, but in the 12th century towers appeared, like those where poor Rapunzel was kept a prisoner.

> **Comment []:**
> Pauline Erlinger-Ford 10/14/16, 6:23 PM
> Do you mean the "ninth century AD?" If so, it should be written that way.

---

[4] At a certain stage, the Holy Roman Empire consisted of approximately 1,800 territories or tiny estates.

Johnny Gruelle's illustration depicting Rapunzel

At a socioeconomic level, some common elements in fairy tales are the existence of families with many children (almost always in extreme poverty), the destitution of the youngest son (since the firstborn used to be the one who got the inheritance), the sacred value of promises (in a time when most people couldn't write and there were no legal contracts), and the dangers of the forest compared to the relative safety of the city or village. "Behind (fairy tales) gorgeous surface, you can glimpse an entire history of childhood and the family: the oppression of landowners and rulers, foundlings, drowsed or abandoned children, the ragamuffin orphan surviving by his wits, the maltreated child who wants a day off from unending toil, or the likely lad who has his eye on a girl who's from a better class than himself, the dependence of old people, the rivalries between competitors for love and other sustenance." (Warner, 2014).

It was in this world of poverty, illiteracy, de-urbanization, loss of Church influence, invasions of Germanic and Scandinavian chiefs, and the emergence of many kingdoms that fairy tales took their current form. They were probably told freely around the fire or meeting places after tedious days, each time adding new details, and since they were a form of entertainment for adults, they were stories full of sex and violence, economic hardship, and premature widowhood or orphanhood. Fairy tales "depict the brutal world of the peasant, with no real view of childhood in mind. Nor is there any trace of sympathetic, patient narration by parents or guardians." (Buch, 2008).

> **Comment []:**
> Pauline Erlinger-Ford 10/14/16, 6:32 PM
> Do you need to have "fairy tales" in brackets here? And it would sound better as "Behind the fairy tales' gorgeous surface…" I realize this is a quote and is quoted correctly so it should not be modified.

> **Comment []:**
> Pauline Erlinger-Ford 10/14/16, 6:37 PM
> Is this the correct word here?

In the modern era, with the Industrial Revolution at full steam, many noticed with concern that urbanization was burying the oral traditions that had existed in their countries for centuries. It was a French storyteller named Catherine Barneville who first used the term "fairy tale," but the honor to be considered the genre's grandfather went to her compatriot Charles Perrault with his *Histoires ou contes du temps passé*, which depicted a kind of gracious king that sent his creation to walk an enchanted and winding road that hasn't finished yet.[5]

> **Comment []:**
> Pauline Erlinger-Ford 10/14/16, 6:47 PM
> Is she commonly known as "Catherine Barneville" because I found that she was called "Marie-Catherine Le Jumel de Barneville."

Barneville

---

[5] Before Perrault, Straparola's Nights was published. It was a collection of ten stories taken from the oral tradition "from the lips of ten girls"; it contained stories similar to those of the Brothers Grimm. Sixty years before Perrault's volume, The Pentamerone also appeared, written by a certain Basile who captured old versions of Cinderella, Rapunzel, Sleeping Beauty and Hansel and Gretel.

A Literary Genre is Born

"Is it you, my Prince?" said she to him. "You have waited a long while." - Sleeping *Beauty*

The literary genre known as "fairy tales" may have been born a few decades before 1697, but the universal agreement is that its father was Perrault, a former adviser to the court of Louis XIV and member of the French Academy who published *Histoires ou Contes du Temps passé* five years before he died. The publication of the small volume of folktales, today considered the genre´s cornerstone, brought new recognition to a writer whose best times were well in the past. When it was published, Perrault was 70 and had just lost his job at the king's court, where he had held a modest but influential position. On one occasion, he suggested to the "Sun King" that the monarch should install fountains of animals in the gardens of Versailles in remembrance of Aesop's fables, a wish that was granted to him. The king also approved Perrault´s request to open the space to the public, a policy that continues to date.

Louis XIV

Although Perrault wrote many "learned" books, he published the volume that gave him immortality under a pseudonym - his son´s name - for fear of ridicule. The stories were already known, and, as discussed above, had probably circulated for centuries, but the book was an unprecedented success, and soon every theater in Paris was making adaptations. Perrault took old stories but left his own touches, adding details that would please the aristocracy of France: more romance, humor and niceties that weren't in the oral versions. For example, in *Cendrillon ou La petite Pantoufle de Verre* (Cinderella) the general opinion among scholars is that the glass slipper and the pumpkin coach were Perrault's creations. In his edition of the complete stories of Perrault, translator Neil Philips explains how the French writer entertained the "jaded audience at the sumptuous court of Louis XIV of France (…) with the simple stories of the people. He gave the tales a more courtly dress and a more knowing air than they would have had in a peasant's cottage, but he did not make fun of them or spoil them with literary embroidery. He let them speak for themselves, and in the process revealed that what they had to say was not so simple after all." (Perrault, 1999).

> **Comment []:** Pauline Erlinger-Ford 10/14/16, 7:25 PM
> Your previous sources have been placed before the full stop.

Perrault's stories are raw and more humorous than the ones known today, and thus were probably closer to the oral tradition, which did not originally have children in mind. When Sleeping Beauty marries the prince, Perrault describes the wedding night with a wink: "They slept, but little," adding later that the prince was afraid of his mother because she was from a race of ogres. After passing the "small foot test," Cinderella is presented to the prince dressed in rags, and the boy "thought she was more charming than before."
Little Red Riding Hood is in Perrault's telling a cautionary tale that the French author wrote to warn of the danger of letting girls go out alone because of the many homeless people and other unsavory types who were on the loose. In his version, the wolf convinces the absent-minded girl to go to bed with him, and when they are together, the wolf "ate her all up." And to leave no doubt about the purpose of the story, he adds at the end: "Moral: Children, especially attractive, well-bred young ladies, should never talk to strangers, for if they should do so, they may well provide dinner for a wolf. I say *wolf*, but there are various kinds of wolves. There are also those who are charming, quiet, polite, unassuming, complacent, and sweet, who pursue young women at home and in the streets. And unfortunately, it is these gentle wolves who are the most dangerous ones of all."

> **Comment []:** Pauline Erlinger-Ford 10/14/16, 7:29 PM
> Homeless what?

As for *Sleeping Beauty*, the story follows the well-known script, but the tale does not end with the kiss breaking off the enchanted sleep. After the wedding, the prince returns to his castle but keeps it secret that he has married the Sleeping Beauty. For two years he is frequently absent from home because he goes to visit his young wife. During that time they procreate twins, two girls called Dawn and Day. However, the prince's mother suspects that her son is up to something. When the old king finally dies, the prince reveals his marital status and enters the castle with his wife and two daughters. The ogress, burning with jealousy, orders the baker to cook the children for her to eat them. The cook pities the children and serves the queen two small deers. When the woman realizes what has happened, she takes Sleeping Beauty, the girls and the disobedient cook to a pit filled with all kinds of snakes, reptiles and other animals. The prince arrives in time to stop the execution. When she is caught in the act, the ogress queen throws herself in the pit to find a horrible death. "The king could not but be very sorry," Perrault ends, "for she was his mother; but he soon comforted himself with his beautiful wife and his pretty children."

As surprising as those origins of the two famous fairy tales are, there is an even scarier example in Perrault´s collection, the much discussed and grisly *Bluebeard*, one of the few stories that has completely disappeared from children´s books. Its bloody events aren´t too distant from gory horror films. Third in the collection, the tale is about a wealthy man who has the misfortune of having a horrible blue beard, "which made him so frightfully ugly that all the women and girls ran away from him." But that was not all. The important thing is that the man with the indigo beard had married several times, and no one knew what had become of his wives. At one point, Bluebeard wins the love of a young woman whom he marries. They get along so well that she thinks the poor man has only been defamed. A month after the wedding, Bluebeard has to go out on a journey. Before leaving, he hands his wife the keys to all his cabinets, chests and the rooms of the luxurious mansion, but he warns that, under no circumstance, can she use the smallest key, which leads to a door at the end of a large alley. She explores the whole house and is amazed, but her curiosity gets the best of her and she opens the forbidden room. Perrault wrote, "(She) opened it, trembling, but could not at first see anything plainly, because the windows were shut. After some moments she began to perceive that the floor was all covered over with clotted blood, on which lay the bodies of several dead women, ranged against the walls. These were all the wives whom Bluebeard had married and murdered, one after another." The young wife flees in terror, but to her great horror she realizes that the key has a blood stain, and since it was a magic key, the stain won´t go away even after repeated washing. Upon his return, Bluebeard demands the key and when she doesn´t deliver it, he becomes enraged, aware that his wife has disobeyed him. Furious, he lets her know that now she´ll take her place among the corpses hanging in the room. The woman begs for a moment to say her last prayers. Bluebeard agrees, but when he can´t wait any longer, he goes upstairs to get her, raises his sword and is about to cut off her head when her brothers come unexpectedly and save her. Hermann Vogel, a German artist of the 19th century, made a horrifying illustration for *Bluebeard*, as creepy as the real story that supposedly inspired the tale.

Vogel's work

Much more amiable are *Puss in Boots*, *Diamonds and Toes*, *Riquet with the Tuft* and *Tom Thumb*. The next three editions also included *Griselidis*, *The Ridiculous Wishes* and *Donkeyskin*, in verse.

Although Perrault's stories were met with widespread approval, the great intellectuals of his time weren't so enthusiastic. They dismissed them as superstitions of the underclass that only served to brutalize people. It would take centuries for the tales of Perrault —later illustrated by great artists like Gustave Doré— to be considered good presents and reading material for children. But the disdain of those who determined what constituted "high literature," the popularity of fairy tales would only increase exponentially.

Dore

A Certain Father Had Two Sons

"But she could not get her big toe into it, the shoe was too small for her. Then her mother gave her a knife and said: Cut the toe off, when you are queen you will have no more need to go on foot." - Cinderella

In the first 15 years of the 19th century, the lands that eventually became Germany were under French rule, but in 1814, shortly before Napoleon's loss at Waterloo, the German Confederation emerged as a conglomeration of 39 small independent states. It was in this context and against this backdrop that the brothers Jacob and Wilhelm Grimm collected, rewrote and then published a collection of stories that to date are one of the pillars of the German literary culture, and once constituted a point of national integration. The brothers were born in Hanau in 1785 and 1786 respectively, and just like the characters of their famous tales, they grew up in extreme poverty. They worked on various literary projects, including a dictionary that they couldn´t finish, but their name became intrinsically linked to their collection of fairy tales, stories that had circulated in Germany for centuries among the people. In doing so, they set the basis and methodology of folklore studies.

To date, the *Tales of the Brothers Grimm* is the best sold book in Germany, second only to the Bible. It has been translated into 140 languages and reached 30 million editions. The original 1812 edition included 86 classics like *Rapunzel, Little Snow-White* and *Cinderella*, albeit with significant variations. In later years they prepared new expanded editions that contained more than 200 stories.

The aim of the Grimm brothers went beyond light entertainment for children. When they began collecting typical German stories, they were trying to recapture everything that contributed to the strengthening of German identity. Germanic studies expert Maria Tatar has called the work of the Brothers Grimm a form of "intellectual resistance" against foreign domination. In 1806, Jacob and Wilhelm began collecting stories from various sources, including peasants, family and aristocratic friends whom they invited to their house. They also visited several regions of Germany although their work focused primarily in Hesse.

Although they weren't very explicit with their sources, it is known that one of their greatest sources of information was a woman called Dorothea Viehmann, whom the brothers met at a very advanced age. Another prominent source was Wilhelm's wife, who heard various tales from her family and the nursemaid. From them, the brothers got *Briar-Rose* (their version of Sleeping Beauty) and *Gretel* (later known as *Hansel and Gretel*). Other sources included a retired sergeant named Friedrich Krause, a pastor of Köteberg, a collector of used clothes, and several members of the Eichsfeld and Droste-Hülshoff Haxthausen families.

In the preface to the first edition of *Kinder-und Hausmärchen,* the brothers asserted that most of the stories came from peasants and townspeople, and that they had captured them in the original form and spirit. They recanted this statement in the second edition, but either way, the book, rightly recognized as a literary and academic portent, received much criticism when it was released. The brothers may have contributed to the formation of a German identity, but when they presented their stories as children's literature, they were criticized because the stories were cruel, glorified violence, and in some cases had sexual content and morally questionable practices. Young Rapunzel, for example, locked deep in the forest on the top of a tower, becomes pregnant after repeated visits by her valiant prince. "Tell me, mother Gothel," she asks her captor, "why are my clothes getting tighter?" In *Little Snow-White*, the wicked queen is not a stepmother but her biological mother, who dies of jealousy because of her beautiful daughter, and even hires a hunter to kill her. "The Grimm Brothers' version of *Snow White* is not only the most popular but also the most homicidal," writes Michelle Ann Abate, a professor of Children's Literature at the University of Ohio. "The jealous stepmother[6] in the tale kills the beautiful title

---

[6] She becomes a stepmother in further editions.

character not once but three times: first, by suffocating her with staylaces; next, by brushing her hair with an enchanted lethal comb; and, finally, by feeding her a poisoned apple."

Alexander Zick's depiction of Snow White

In another story, *The Children of Famine*, a mother, desperate due to poverty, announces to her daughters, "You've got to die or else we'll waste away." The children offer her slices of bread, but she can't satisfy her hunger. As a last resort, the mother suggests that they sleep "until the Judgment Day arrives," which the girls do, but not her, who disappears forever without a trace.

In the Grimm brothers' version of *Cinderella*, there is no Fairy Godmother (which they considered too French), but the spirit of the dead mother and a magic tree; the tale repeats the shoe motif and has a prince willing to marry the girl whose foot it fits. But in this version, Cinderella's stepmother tells one of her daughters:, "Here's a knife ... if the slipper is still too tight for you, then a cut off a piece of your foot. It will hurt a bit. But what does that matter." It is only when the prince's envoy sees the blood dripping from the shoe that he realizes the mutilated woman is not the one he's looking for.

> **Comment []:**
> Pauline Erlinger-Ford 10/15/16, 7:35 AM
> The smallest what? Something is missing here and by adding it, will make this story easier to understand.

Anne Anderson's illustration of Cinderella

Perhaps the most disturbing example in the Grimm brothers' collection is a small tale entitled *How Some Children Played at Slaughtering*. The story is about a group of little children playing gastronomy, where one is the butcher, another the cook, and another the kitchen assistant. The smallest happens to be the little pig, so his playmates slice his throat with a knife. The mother, who is bathing her baby, hears the cry and runs to see what happens. When she watches the macabre spectacle, she pulls the knife out of the dead boy and in a fit of rage nails it in the oldest son's chest. While she does that, however, the baby is left unattended in the bathtub and drowns.

When the mother goes back inside the house and sees her, she hangs herself in despair. As if all that wasn't enough, in the afternoon the father returns home after a hard day of work in the field, only to see his entire family dead. He dies of sadness.

Many readers were naturally concerned with the blood orgy, so the Grimm brothers had to prepare new editions over the years. The versions most people know today are different from those in the first edition, which remained in the German language for centuries and were only translated into English in 2012. In the preface to the second edition, Wilhelm acknowledged their literary contribution in the stories and began to clean up the gory details and set aside the rawest narratives until they were almost completely forgotten. They replaced the mothers for stepmothers, as in *Little Snow-White*. The Grimm brothers yielded to social pressure in a time when motherhood was considered to be sacred, but their stories certainly depicted a rather common situation: the high mortality rate during childbirth and hence the abundance of stepmothers. "Many stories explore threats all too familiar to the stories´ receivers: The loss of a mother in childbirth is a familiar, melancholy opening to many favourites." (Warner, 2014). As with Perrault, there has been a lot of debate regarding to what extent the Brothers Grimm presented their stories as told by the people, and how much is owed to their own creativity. Clearly, the siblings homogenized the literary style in all their stories, but apparently they also composed new ones using snippets of incomplete tales since their work began at a time when the oral tradition was already being lost. In a letter to a colleague, Wilhelm Grimm acknowledged that during their field research, the brothers found that many stories survived in a fragmentary state, and that the most prominent trait was the beginning or plot of the narratives. That is probably the way many were circulating at the time.[7] The surprisingly similar endings were perhaps the brothers´ creation.

In the second edition of *Kinder-und Hausmärchen*, Jacob and Wilhelm presented not only sterilized versions, they also expanded the anthology and got rid of some stories that they suspected had originated in France. Interestingly, they didn´t remove *Little Red Cap* (Perrault´s *Little Red Riding Hood)*, which they considered the "typical German narrative."
In the seventh and final edition, published in 1857, the brothers wrote, "We removed in this edition any expression that is not suitable for childhood." The versions in this release, some with Christian elements like angels and proverbs, are the basis for all editions and translations made after the brothers´ deaths in 1859 (Wilhelm) and 1863 (Jacob). "Had Wilhelm Grimm not revised and restored the tales, no one other than a handful of philologists and narrative researchers would have heard of them today." (McGlathery, 1991). By this time, about 50 stories had been removed or rewritten. The stories of the first edition are, however, where the voice of the people and the oral tradition resonate more clearly.

---

[7] For example, a basic story would be: "Once a witch locked a princess in a tower in the middle of a forest, but a prince found the tower and impregnated the girl".

In Search of the Historical Characters
"Think of every fairy-tale villainess you've ever heard of. Think of the wicked witches, the evil queens, the mad enchantresses. Think of the alluring sirens, the hungry ogresses, the savage she-beasts. Remember that somewhere, sometime, they've all been real." - Jim Butcher

Although some still see fairy tales as inferior or entry-level literature because their characters are one-dimensional - the bad are so evil, and princesses are so beautiful - many primary impulses can be found in their pages. *Snow White* illustrates the deadly jealousy among rival women, Bluebeard's wife portrays the dangers of curiosity, and the princess in *Riquet with the Tuft* is perhaps a prototype of the dumb blonde. But is there an extra layer behind those colorful characters? Yes and no. Millions of cinderellas have lived in all ages —there are similar stories in China, North Africa and the Native American Indians of girls who fall into the clutches of unsavory characters and disappointed children who receive a meager inheritance. However, others like Bluebeard, Snow White and the stupid king in *The Emperor's New Clothes* are so conspicuous that it's valid to ask whether they are based on historical characters, even if only loosely.

> **Comment []:**
> Pauline Erlinger-Ford 10/15/16, 8:06 AM
> How about "Cinderellas" instead of just cinderellas.

Vilhelm Pederson's illustration of the emperor with no clothes

Studies on *Snow White and the Seven Dwarfs* could occupy an entire section in university libraries. For decades, historians and folklorists have searched for the princess in history books. As noted above, there were clear similarities between Snow White and the German princess Margaretha von Waldeck, who may not even be the best candidate for the historical Snow White, if there was one. Worthy of consideration is also Maria Sophia von Erthal, a girl born in 1729 in the village of Lohr am Main, a part of Germany characterized by its thick forests. According to the records, she was the daughter of a noble or royal bureaucrat named Phillip Christoph von Erthal. His wife died when Maria was still a child. The nobleman got married again in 1743 to Claudia Elisabeth von Reichenstein, a dominant and embittered woman who brought children from a previous marriage. The lady —but of course! — abhorred her teenage stepdaughter of 14.

Maria Sophia von Erthal

The entire region where Lohr is located can be the key for identification. Besides the great forests, the region was once an important mining area. As in the story of Margaretha von Waldeck, Lohr miners were mostly children or adults suffering from dwarfism. A source of the time notes that "the physical condition of the boys and girls engaged in the mines is much inferior to that of (other) children of the same age. These children are, upon the whole, prejudicially affected to a material extent in their growth and development; many of them are short for their years." The other notable feature of the region was its production of glass and mirrors of such good quality that people joked that local mirrors "always told the truth." The factories also made some sort of acoustic toys called "talking mirrors." Nobleman Phillip gave one of those truthful mirrors to his second wife, and the piece is still exhibited in the family's castle, which is today the Sepssart Museum.

The Grimm brothers, or the anonymous sources who told them the story, could have also incorporated a poisonous plant of the area, one of the most toxic in Europe, popularly known as Nightlock Berry. The *Atropa belladonna* produces purple berries. A botany book of 1971 describes them as "full of a dark, inky juice and intensely sweet, and their attraction to children on that account, has from their poisonous properties, been attended with fatal results." It would be altogether possible that at some point poor Maria, tired of her stepmother's mistreatment, ran away from home and survived thanks to the hospitality of the crippled miners of the area. Or maybe she died from eating one of the deadly berries.

Although *Rapunzel*, the captive princess who let her lengthy hair fall from the window for the prince to climb is similar to *Persinette*, published in France in 1785, the townsfolk of Trendelburg, Germany claim that the princess really existed and was once a prisoner in a famous tower located in the town. Touristic purposes aside, the most likely explanation is that *Rapunzel* is just a variation of a story about thousands of women who were confined for life, a common practice in many cultures, especially in the case of unlawful sexual intercourse (as suggested by the original version of *Rapunzel*, where the girl becomes pregnant). "Because the association of wives and domestic seclusion existed (in medieval times), grounding a wife at home may have been seen as a suitable disciplinarian measure, to restore chastity and to shield misbehaving women-folk from public sight," writes Julia Hillner, professor of Ancient History at the University of Sheffield. The church also recommended the seclusion of women in order to eradicate the practice of beating them as a disciplinary measure (Hillner, 2015).

More historical credibility has the nightmarish story of *Bluebeard*, the opulent and ugly nobleman whose wives mysteriously disappeared, after he murdered and stacked them in a room at the end of a corridor. The story could preserve traces of the legend of Saint Tryphine, a Christian martyr who lived in the 6th century in Britain. Not much is known about her except that she was the wife of Conomor, a Breton chief who killed her. In later expansions, the legend says that besides Tryphine, Conomor had murdered his other three wives. At first, Tryphine refuses to marry him because of his reputation as a cruel man, but in the end she agrees under the condition that she may go home if she suffers abuse from her husband. According to the legend, Tryphine finds a secret room with relics of the previous wives, whose spirits appear to warn her that the man will kill her if she becomes pregnant.

Paul Barlow's picture of a statue depicting St. Tryphine

The most accepted theory is that *Bluebeard*, first published in France, was modeled after Gilles de Rais, a member of the nobility who fought alongside Joan of Arc in the 15th century. Gilles practiced black magic, and during his trial he confessed to killing children in his rituals. The victims were impoverished kids who came to his castle to ask for food. Gilles opened the door, received them, pampered them ,and dressed them in fine clothes in order to earn their trust. In his house on the northern coast of France, 40 corpses of children were found, although historians believe that he may have killed more than 200.

Gilles de Rais

Just like Bluebeard, Gilles hung his victims on hooks in a secret room before beheading them and raping them through the cavity he had created. He evaded justice for many years because he was influential and nobody dared to doubt his honor, having served France on the battlefield. In his trial, the ex-soldier declared that "when the said children were dead, he kissed them and those who had the most handsome limbs and heads he held up to admire them, and had their bodies cruelly cut open and took delight at the sight of their inner organs; and very often when the children were dying he sat on their stomachs and took pleasure in seeing them die and laughed." (Benedetti, 1971).

Interestingly, Perrault preserves the story of Gilles de Rais in the middle part of *Sleeping Beauty*. When the prince asks who owns the abandoned castle, his companion says that "in the castle lived an ogre, who carried thither all the children whom he could catch. There he devoured them at his leisure, and since he was the only person who could force a passage through the wood, nobody had been able to pursue him."

> **Comment []:**
> Pauline Erlinger-Ford 10/15/16, 11:51 AM
> What do you mean by "through the cavity he had created?"

Henry Meynell Rheam's depiction of Sleeping Beauty

There are many stories about people who become rich or famous thanks to their cat. Richard Whittington was an historical character who lived in the 15th century in England. He was in the textile trade and had such a good fortune that even the king of England borrowed money from him. He was the mayor of London four times and stood out as a great philanthropist.

Legends about his origins and how he became so fabulously rich grew around him. The first "biographies" of Whittington appeared in the 1600s and by then they were already impregnated with legendary details. Some accounts affirmed that young Richard grew up in poverty and went to London to seek his fortune. He found employment with a wealthy merchant who had a pest problem in his house. To alleviate this, Richard bought a cat that eradicated the plague. In one of his frequent trips, the merchant took the cat and sold it for a fortune to a king of the Mediterranean coast of Africa, and this made him incalculably rich. In gratitude, he gave his daughter's hand to young Richard, who went on to become the Mayor of London, and this is perhaps the only authentic historical data. In one contemporary portrait, Whittington is depicted holding a cat. The kitten seems to be winking at viewers, but it doesn't wear boots.

A contemporary depiction of Whittington and his cat

Fairy Tales from Other Kingdoms

"Open, Sesame!" - Ali Baba and the Forty Thieves
The publication of folk stories in Europe didn´t start with Perrault or end with the Brothers Grimm, but the brothers set a precedent by identifying their sources and presenting them in an orderly fashion with stylistic uniformity. They also "improved" the tales with subsequent editions, ultimately cementing the genre and laying the foundation for the discipline now known as Folklore Studies.[8] In the centuries that followed, several scholars and writers from other countries joined the wave unleashed by the Grimm brothers and began to collect folk stories and compose their own fairy tales.

---

[8] A hundred years before Perrault, Giovanni Francesco Straparola published the first identifiable fairy tales, although stylistically they are far from those who came later.

Without a doubt the high mark came with the work of Danish writer Hans Christian Andersen, who started publishing a few years after the Grimm brothers. First, he published the stories he heard as a child, and he later added tales of his own invention that brought the genre to a new artistic grandeur.

Andersen

Andersen had more recognition in life with his novels and poetry, but today his name is inextricably linked to classics like *The Emperor's New Clothes, The Little Mermaid, The Ugly Duckling,* and *The Princess and the Pea*. His first known work, found by chance only in 2012, is called *The Tallow Candle*. Andersen wrote it while he was still in school, and it´s about a candle that can't find meaning in life. "So there was the poor Tallow Candle, solitary and left alone, at a loss at what to do. Rejected by the good, it now realized it had only been a tool to further the wicked. It felt so unbelievably unhappy, because it had spent its life to no good end. It just could not determine why it had been created or where it belonged; why it had been put on this earth." The candle finally finds meaning to existence when it meets a matchbox. "Out burst the flame, like the triumphant torch of a blissful wedding. Light burst out bright and clear all around, bathing the way forward with light for its surroundings —its true friends— who were now able to seek truth in the glow of the candle." After this, Andersen went on to write more than 156 stories.

Hans Christian Andersen was a misunderstood and melancholic artist, a conflicted man who possibly led a double life. He renounced sexuality, but during his life he fervently desired to find love, only to find none. In one of the entries in his diaries, he wrote, "Almighty God, thee only have I; thou steerest my fate, I must give myself up to thee! Give me a livelihood! Give me a bride! My blood wants love, as my heart does!" It's not rare to find this desperation and need for love in his stories. *The Little Mermaid*, one of the most celebrated, is a depressing story in which an unhappy and lovesick mermaid makes a diabolical deal with a sea witch to attain the love of a young prince whom she sees in a ship. The witch offers to make the little mermaid human in exchange for her voice and her condition as a siren (therefore her long life). However, the witch warns, if she fails to win the prince's heart, she will die and dissolve into sea foam. The prince fails to recognize the extent of her sacrifice and marries another woman. The unfortunate protagonist, now a human being, has two paths before her: to die and become foam or regain her status as a siren, which she can only accomplish by killing the prince. The witch herself sends the knife, but the Little Mermaid is unable to murder her beloved and instead throws herself to the sea and dies.

Edmund Dulac's illustration of the Little Mermaid and the prince

Andersen's stories are much more sentimental than Perrault's and the Grimm brothers' fairy tales; they delve deeper in their protagonists' feelings, like in *The Little Match Girl*, and their characters are imbued with the feeling that they have a special destiny. Andersen's "happy endings" are also rather peculiar. In many cases they involve the protagonist's death, who finally arrives in Heaven, as in *The Selfish Giant*. They often include animated objects, such as *The Steadfast Tin Soldier*.

Another essential author is the Russian researcher Alexander Afanasyev, a contemporary of the Brothers Grimm who published nearly 600 short stories between 1855 and 1867. Unlike Andersen, and more like the Grimm brothers, Afanasyev functioned more as a compiler, editor and folklorist than an author, but he went beyond the German brothers because he was more meticulous. During the course of his work, he used to register his sources, the place where he heard the history, the date, and who had told it. Unfortunately, Afanasyev's tales are mostly unknown outside Slavic countries, and they should be in the library of everyone interested in fairy tales. His stories fit the genre perfectly, and at the same time they're unique and fresher than the "classic" tales already debilitated by repetition.

Afanasyev

Some nice examples are *The Princess Who Never Smiled*, whose desperate father offers her hand to the man who can make her laugh. *The Girl Without Arms* is about a deadly quarrel between a young woman and her sister-in-law, to the point that when the latter gives birth, she kills her own baby and blames her rival; the grieving father has to ask her sister to cut off her arms. There is also the especially macabre *Vasilisa the Beautiful*, a girl whose dying mother gives her a tiny magic doll that helps her in desperate situations. The father goes on a long journey and Vasilisa's cruel stepmother takes the whole family to live in a miserable cabin in the woods. On one occasion, she sends the girl to ask for fire from one of the scariest characters in Slavic folklore, Baba Yaga, a witch with chicken feet who lives deep in the forest, in a house lit with glowing skulls and surrounded by a fence made of human bones. Baba Yaga first asks Vasilisa to make several errands before giving her the fire, with the warning that if she fails, she'll have to kill her. The magic doll that Vasilisa keeps in her pocket helps her all the time.

An illustration depicting Vasilisa at the hut of Baba Yaga

Further north, readers can find the wonderful *East of the Sun and West of the Moon*, a Norwegian tale published in the 19th century that is among the best in the canon, and also *The Gifts of the Magician*, an intriguing Finnish fairy tale about a child who gets lost in the woods after following a bird that he intended to kill against his mother's advice.

Europe was hardly the only region with these kinds of tales. Although the plots, landscapes, names and colors vary, in 1706 the publication of *Arabian Nights*, a collection of stories of the Middle East that were gathered along many centuries, came to enrich Western imagination. There is no definitive version of *Arabian Nights*; some editions contain less than a hundred tales and others have more than a thousand, but all are framed in the same main story about King

Shahryar. Embittered after the infidelity and execution of his first wife, the king decides that all women are the same and begins to marry a different maid every night, which he has beheaded at sunrise before she has a chance to dishonor him. When the kingdom runs out of single girls, Scheherazade, the vizier's daughter, offers herself to be the next wife and stop the slaughtering. The bureaucrat refuses, but her daughter asks him to trust her plan. On the wedding night, Scheherazade begins to tell the king a story with such narrative genius that he is fascinated, but the bride is careful enough to stop the story in the middle.

"At this point in her tale," according to *Arabian Nights*, "Shahrazad saw the approach of morning and discreetly fell silent," and tells the king that what he has heard is nothing compared with what she has to tell him the next night if she's still alive. The king thinks, "By Allah, I will not kill her until I have heard the rest of her tale!" The next night, artful Scheherazade ends the story only to begin a more engaging one. The same thing happens for a thousand nights.
Among the best stories, many of which have been brought to the big screen, are *Aladdin and the Wonderful Lamp*, *Ali Baba and the Forty Thieves,* and although not part of the original Arabic edition, the fantastic saga of *Sinbad the Sailor* and his seven journeys. *Arabian Nights* introduces imaginative traits absent from European stories, such as genies coming out of lamps, giant birds whose eggs are as big as rocks, Caliph Harun al-Rashid (a historical figure), caves full of treasures that are opened with magic words, sea monsters, and male witches residing on abandoned islands.

Max Liebert's illustration of Aladdin in the Magic Garden

There is also a collection of Native American folk tales that Mexican anthropologist Anita Brenner heard in the early 20th century from a woman called Luz Jimenez, born in 1897 in Milpa Alta, then a ranch in southern Mexico. "She is an Indian woman who lives in an Indian village in Mexico," Brenner wrote at the beginning of her collection. "Some stories are things that happened in their own town, Milpa Alta. Some are things that the old people say were told to them by their grandfathers and they said it happened a long time ago, and they heard it from their grandfathers. Luz knows more stories than anyone. If you lived in Milpa Alta, you could sit around the fire and hear her tell a different story every night until you were as old as your grandfather." (Brenner, 1942). Anita Brenner was with Luz Jimenez in the 1930s, and the stories were published under the title *The Boy Who Could Do Anything*. The names of the tales are

> **Comment []:**
> Pauline Erlinger-Ford 10/15/16, 5:50 PM
> You are repeating yourself here. Has the quote been correctly quoted?

intriguing: *The Boy Who Beat the Devil*, *The Dead Man That Was Alive* and *Maria Sat on the Fire*.

Luz Jimenez, who was also a source for linguists who were studying the Nahuatl language, served as a model for artist Diego Rivera — she appears in at least three of his murals — and was immortalized in the Fountain of Cántaros in Mexico City. She was hit by a car and died in 1965 at the age of 68, but only after having told her life´s story to anthropologist Fernando Horcasitas.

In 1902, less than two years after the death of Oscar Wilde, perhaps the last great writer of "fairy tales," journalist L. Frank Baum wrote for the *Chicago Evening Post* that he saw no impediment to the emergence of another Hans Christian Andersen "to bless children with a modern collection of original fairy tales."

Discounting the multiple modernized counterparts of the Grimm stories, such as the erotic and second-rate versions of Snow White or Cinderella, what is the current state of the genre? It´s always difficult to set clear boundaries between fairy tale, legend, and mythology, but it's fair to say that the genre gained force in the 20th century. In 1911 *Peter and Wendy*, a novel featuring Peter Pan and probably the most famous fairy of all time, Tinker Bell, was published in London. Between 1950 and 1955, C.S. Lewis wrote the *Chronicles of Narnia*, three novels including both elements of historical fiction (the story begins in England during World War II), as well as elements of fairy tales, notably a witch, a talking lion, an enchanted kingdom ,and a magical wardrobe that transports children to a different world (just like the trap on the floor in *The Twelve Dancing Princesses)*. More recently, authors like Michael Ende and Neil Gaiman could be regarded too as gifted writers of fairy tales. *Coraline* and *Momo* belong to that world as much as *Rapunzel* or *Hansel and Gretel* did.

Francis Donkin Bedford's illustration of Peter Pan playing pipes in Never Never Land

Are Fairy Tales Good for Children
"Even fairy tales, the ones we all love, with wizards or princesses turning into frogs or whatever it was… There's a very interesting reason why a prince could not turn into a frog – it's statistically too improbable." - Richard Dawkins

The direct and simple themes of fairy tales, common to every person on the planet —domestic jealousy, unrequited love, desire for wealth, anxiety about marriage— constituted an excellent reason for others to have a go at the genre. Many of these people subsequently adapted them to other media. On numerous occasions, theater, radio and cinema tailored the most celebrated fairy tales. Perhaps no one can rival Disney Studios in bringing the stories to millions of children. It's no exaggeration to affirm that since the mid-20th century, many children recognized Disney as the source of fairy tales, not Perrault or the Brothers Grimm.

The work of the Brothers Grimm was collected at a stage in which intellectuals were trying to recover and revalue German culture. Therefore, German nationalism put their eyes on their work in the 20th century. The dark side was the use of fairy tales as political propaganda and racist brainwashing, which proves that any material in the wrong hands can be used for misguided purposes. In Germany, National Socialism soon glimpsed the potential of fairy tales to indoctrinate children, and from a very early stage leaders began to use them to spread Nazi ideology. One of the first films was *Puss in Boots*, directed by Lotte Reiniger. At the end of the film the cat morphs into a figure resembling Hitler who is cheered by the crowds: "He is our Savior, we will live again."

That was not all. In 1939, the year of Germany's invasion of Poland, *Little Red Riding* Hood premiered in Germany, and in this adaptation the girl wears a shawl with a swastika as she moves through the forest and is saved from the wolf by a man in a SS uniform. In Alfred Stöger's adaptation of *The Magic Table, The Donkey and the Golden Club in the Sack!*, a farmer is threatened to be punished with a "yellow mark" on his blue pants. In Germany, the "yellow mark" was used to identify and single out Jews. German producer Hubert Schonger, who was favorable to Nazism, said in the mid-1930s, "Every fairy tale is politically alignable without raping the poetry within," although propaganda chief Joseph Goebbels himself warned not be too heavy handed: "Children will see through advertising quicker than their parents ever could."

After World War II, the Allies immediately banned the use of Grimm's fairy tales in German schools, withdrew all copies from libraries, and sent them to American universities. The tales of Jacob and Wilhelm were forgotten for some time, and although they're still held in high esteem, Germany hasn't fully reconciled with the past. Louis Snyder, an American academic who witnessed the rise of Hitler firsthand, wrote that the brothers' tales had contributed to the formation of many vices in the German temperament, such as obedience, authoritarianism, the glorification of violence, and nationalism. Writer Matthias Matussek echoed this sentiment in an essay published not long ago in *Der Spiegel*, arguing that the most successful book in the German language "offered an unparalleled exploration into the (German) people's dark souls."

Understandably, psychoanalysts eventually became interested in fairy tales. Sigmund Freud and his followers eagerly analyzed the stories and interpreted them as they did with dreams. Viewing the stories in symbolic terms, psychoanalysts interpreted them as liberating stories for children, especially in their relationships with their parents. A typical Freudian analysis, for example, would see the red cap in *Little Red Riding Hood* as a symbol of menstruation, the wolf as a representation of repressed desire, the hunter as a father figure, and the stones that filled the animal's belly as a pregnancy (or according to Eric Fromm, one of Freud's disciples, the triumph of the misanthropic woman who punishes the male figure with a symbolic pregnancy). And while it's likely that below fairy tales run deep waters, psychological analysis of fairy tales is a kind of Rorschach test. Everyone sees what they want, so it´s not uncommon that each psychoanalyst could come up with a completely different interpretation.

This obsession to observe fairy tales with a magnifying glass continued throughout the 20th century. Even though the Brothers Grimm purified the first versions of their stories, during the 20th century educators frowned again on much of their work. Some commented that the stories still contained a great amount of violence, especially against women, though in a veiled way. Meanwhile, feminists complained about the negative role of women in fairy tales (evil, dumb, vindictive, naive, jealous, or abused), while men are usually benevolent or absent.
In some cases, political correctness reached extremes. In 1989, two California school districts banned *Little Red Riding Hood* from the classroom because the story says that the girl was carrying cake and wine for her grandmother. In 1994, every Brothers Grimm tale was banned in Arizona for children under 12 due to their "excessive violence and negative portrayals of female characters."

Perhaps the Brothers Grimm themselves are responsible for the anger of feminists, with their overpopulation of silly and passive heroines. In 2009, for example, another collection made in the mid-19th century by a German man named Franz Xaver von Schönwerth was discovered. Inspired by his countrymen, Schönwerth began to collect stories, lullabies, and proverbs in villages of Bavaria that the people shared with him in exchange for coffee and cigarettes. Schönwerth was unknown in his time, but scholars today emphasize the "authenticity and freshness" of his stories. They are "raw [and] uncooked," in the words of expert Maria Tatar.

Here women are not so badly portrayed. In *King Goldilocks,* it is a boy who is taken to the woods to be killed by a hunter, who must return with his lungs and heart; the youngster who must sleep with a frog in bed is a boy named Jodl; and in *The Three Princesses* the heroine is a woman. In the final confrontation, the brave girl takes a sword and turns into a lake, makes the witch drink all the water, and then cuts the witch´s womb and emerges with her sword to save her prince, whom she decides to marry. Schönwerth reveals "the degree to which the Grimms were selective in terms of gender, favoring stories about beautiful persecuted heroines and bold heroes."[9]
Outside Germany, there are examples of bold heroines too. In *East of the Sun and West of the Moon*, a Norwegian tale, it´s the defenseless prince who tells the girl: "You alone can save me," for he has to marry a troll woman with a long nose.[10] In the end the girl defeats the trolls, stops the wedding and keeps the prince. Perhaps the Grimms were too heavy handed.

> Comment []:
> Pauline Erlinger-Ford 10/15/16, 8:43 PM
> I cannot verify the spelling of this name.

---

[9] The Anti-Grimm, retrieved on September 26, 2016 from:
http://www.economist.com/blogs/prospero/2012/04/fairy-tales

[10] In Scandinavian folklore, a troll is a supernatural being dangerous for humans. They live in

The Interpretation of Fairy Tales

"That is why it is so extremely important to tell children fairytales (...) because they are instrumental symbols with whose help unconscious contents can be canalized into consciousness, interpreted, and integrated." - Carl Gustav Jung

In *East of the Sun and West of the Moon*, a white bear arrives at the house of an impoverished family in a dark and stormy night (before it was a literary cliché) and asks the householder to give him his youngest daughter in exchange for untold riches. When she agrees, the white bear asks her politely climb on its back and runs away through the snow. "Are you afraid?" the bear asks several times in the story, to which the heroine always says no. The girl literally clings to her husband, who will protect her in her symbolic journey of passage from childhood to adulthood.

Is it possible to find meanings like this, or meanings of any kind, from fairy tales? The purpose is not new. Charles Perrault himself came up with an interpretation at the end of each story. In the last page of *Cinderella,* he wrote, "Beauty in a woman is a rare treasure that will always be admired. Graciousness, however, is priceless and of even greater value. This is what Cinderella's godmother gave to her when she taught her to behave like a queen. Young women, in the winning of a heart, graciousness is more important than a beautiful hairdo. It is a true gift of the fairies." At the end of *Bluebeard,* he warned, "Curiosity, in spite of its appeal, often leads to deep regret. To the displeasure of many a maiden, its enjoyment is short lived." The immediate interpretation, and perhaps a correct one, is that fairy tales are cautionary tales to warn people about the dangers of leaving the city, to value people not according to their physical appearance, and to alert readers that luck can change suddenly, for bad or good, because fairies are capricious.

These simple interpretations don't necessarily exclude others. Beyond the obvious moral of the story, it's the psychoanalytic vision which has attracted most fascination. "Fairy tales," writes Marie-Louis von Franz, a disciple of Jung, "are the purest and simplest expression of collective unconscious psychic processes. Therefore their value for the scientific investigation of the unconscious exceeds that of all other material. They represent the archetypes in their simplest, barest and most concise form." It's no coincidence that most fairy tales begin with the words "Once upon a time." That is, they don't happen at any special time or place. (Von Franz, 1996). Fairy tales may be historically empty, but they are emotionally helpful.

Since their publication, editors and the public have been attracted to the recurring themes of fairy tales, including jealous stepmothers, shape-changing husbands, dangerous forests, enchanted dreams and animals helpers, just to name a few. In the 20th century there were at least two

---

remote places and haven't been Christianized.

serious attempts to answer the question of why the same themes were repeated. One school of thought was that fairy tales speak of ancient agricultural myths (the death of the sun, the seasons) and another, much more successfully, asserted that fairy tales were originally derived from recurring dreams common to all mankind (being lost in the woods, being chased by an animal, people changing shape, etc.) that form part of the collective unconscious. On the contrary, a Marxist would argue that *Snow White* is a denunciation of the hardships of the working class, which survives only because of their solidarity, and that stories where people desire the prince's happiness are propaganda to convince the proletariat that the welfare of the upper classes is convenient for everybody.

Two quotes that explain the constant fascination with fairy tales are attributed to G. K. Chesterton, one of the most prolific writers who ever lived. "Fairy tales do not tell children dragons exist. Children already know that dragons exist. Fairy tales tell children the dragons can be killed." In doing so, Chesterton takes sides with the school that says that fairy tales have therapeutic value since they teach children important truths about life and how to overcome adversity. After all, powerful men are not always the most intelligent, as *The Emperor's New Clothes* makes abundantly clear, and a real princess will always be one even if she's dressed in rags. Those who look monstrous are not always detestable. In *Beauty and the Beast* it's quite clear that someone must first be loved before being lovable.

In 1976, child psychologist Bruno Bettelheim published one of the seminal studies of the interpretation of fairy tales, *The Uses of Enchantment: The Meaning and Importance of Fairy Tales*. Despite their dark characters and crude situations, Bettelheim defends the value of fairy tales because children can interpret and process them their own way, and thus symbolically resolve their fears and release their emotions. "The child intuitively comprehends that although these stories are unreal, they are not untrue," emphasizes Bettelheim, adding, "The fairy tales' concern is not useful information about the external world, but the inner process taking place in an individual." In other words, fairy tales are about how to grow up and how to pass the stages of life, and they offer warnings that some places are better left alone and uncrossed. "Even if we are persuaded, as I am, that fairy tales are somehow real documents of the past," writes scholar Marina Warner, "we don't need to know anything about the Black Forest to recognize ourselves in the plots of *Red Riding Hood, Sleeping Beauty or Hansel* and *Gretel*." (2014).

One doesn't have to be a psychiatrist to see the subtle but clear message in the corners of the Grimm brothers' universe. Like Snow White's stepmother, at some point people all have to face the mirror. Everyone gets lost eventually in some dark forest, "the place in which inner darkness is confronted and worked through; where uncertainty is resolved about who one is; and where one begins to understand who one wants to be." (Bettelheim, 1976). Perhaps aware of this, C. S. Lewis wrote to his goddaughter, Lucy Barfield, in the dedication of *The Lion, the Witch and the Wardrobe*, "My Dear Lucy, I wrote this story for you, but when I began it I had not realized that girls grow quicker than books. As a result you are already too old for fairy tales, and by the time it is printed and bound, you will be older still. But some day you will be old enough to start reading fairy tales again. You can then take it down from some upper shelf, dust it, and tell me what you think of it. I shall probably be too deaf to hear, and too old to understand a word you say, but I shall still be your affectionate Godfather."

Lewis, one of the most celebrated British intellectuals of the 20th century, was also a troubled soul who spent his life in search of truth and happiness, going from atheism to realism to Christianity, always considering reason to be his most appreciated value. His life was an "intricate journey through the worlds of thought and feeling and desire; his passionate search for truth (…) a picture of genuine mystical experience, rationalized by philosophy."

Is it a coincidence that in the prologue of his most widely read work, he aspired to write a great fairy tale? Maybe Lewis knew something others didn't.

Bibliography

Andersen, Hans C., (2014), *Hans Christian Andersen's Complete Fairy Tales*. England: Canterbury Classics.

Benedetti, Jean (1971), *Gilles de Rais*, New York, USA: Stein and Day.

Brenner, Anita, (1992). *The Boy Who Could Do Anything & Other Mexican Folktales: And Other Mexican Folktales*. USA: Linnet Books.

Buch, David J., (2008). *Magic Flutes and Enchanted Forests: The Supernatural in Eighteenth-Century Musical Theater*. USA: University Of Chicago Press.

Creighton, Oliver, (2005). *Castles and Landscapes: Power, Community and Fortification in Medieval England*. Great Britain: Equinox.

Grimm Jacob, Wilhelm *et al* (2014). *The Original Folk and Fairy Tales of the Brothers Grimm: The Complete First Edition*. USA: Princeton University Press.

Hillner, Julia, (2015). *Prison, Punishment and Penance in Late Antiquity*. USA: Cambridge University Press.

McGlathery, James *et al*, (1991). *The Brothers Grimm and Folktale*. USA: University of Illinois Press; Reprint edition.

Perrault, Charles; Philip, Neil; *et al* (1993). *The Complete Fairy Tales of Charles Perrault*. USA: Clarion Books.

Pilkington, Olga *et al.* (2010). *Fairy Tales of the Russians and Other Slavs*. Forest Tsar Press.

Tatar, Maria, (2002). *The Annotated Classic Fairy Tales.* USA: W. W. Norton & Company.

Von Franz, Marie, (1996), *The Interpretation of Fairy Tales*. Boston: Shambhala.

Warner, Marina, (2014). *Once upon a time. A short history of fairy tale.* UK: Oxford University Press.

Free Books by Charles River Editors

We have brand new titles available for free most days of the week. To see which of our titles are currently free, click on this link.

Discounted Books by Charles River Editors

We have titles at a discount price of just 99 cents everyday. To see which of our titles are currently 99 cents, click on this link.

Printed in Great Britain
by Amazon